# DreamTeam

"your dreams delivered"

## Mission 2: Showtime

## Ann Coburn

*For Gill Evans,*
*who shared the dream*

First published 2006 by Walker Books Ltd
87 Vauxhall Walk, London SE11 5HJ

2 4 6 8 10 9 7 5 3 1

Text © 2006 Ann Coburn
Illustrations © 2006 Garry Parsons

The right of Ann Coburn and Garry Parsons to be identified
as author and illustrator respectively of this work has been
asserted by them in accordance with the Copyright, Designs
and Patents Act 1988

This book has been typeset in Stone Informal

Printed in and bound in Great Britain by Creative Print and
Design (Wales), Ebbw Vale

British Library Cataloguing in Publication Data:
a catalogue record for this book is available
from the British Library

ISBN-13: 978-1-8442-8071-1
ISBN-10: 1-84428-071-3

www.walkerbooks.co.uk

# Contents

# Showtime

## "Attention, trainees!"

The Dream Centre was busy and full
of noise. Steam and shouts erupted
from the Dream Kitchens. The airspace
between the line of launch pads and the
gateway was full of dreamskoots taking
off or coming in to land. But even the
whine of dreamskoots could not drown

out Team Leader Flint. Her voice soared over the launch pads, loud and clear.

Vert, Midge, Snaffle and Harley scurried onto the metal walkway at the back of their launch pads. It was not wise to keep Team Leader Flint waiting. They lined up and stood to attention with their helmets tucked under their arms. This was an important day for their dream

team. Basic training was over, but to become fully qualified Dream Fetchers they had to fly four Earthside missions. The first mission, a solo dream delivery, had been completed and they each wore one stripe on the sleeve of their uniform to prove it. Now the day of the second mission had arrived. They were about to take the navigation test.

Team Leader Flint began her inspection, checking everything from helmets to boots. Vert was first in line. He sucked in his stomach and held his breath. His jacket was straining a bit across the front and he did not want Team Leader Flint to notice. Vert kept his stomach in until Team Leader Flint moved on, then he sagged like an old balloon.

Midge was next. She went up on her toes and stretched her neck, trying to look as tall as she could while Team Leader Flint looked her over. Midge was always conscious of her height at times like this. Dream Fetchers were supposed to be at least seven centimetres tall and she was only six and three quarters. Midge had lost count of the number of times she had been turned down for Dream Fetcher training, but she had kept coming back until, finally, Team Leader Flint had said yes. Now Midge was exactly where she wanted to be, but she worried that Team Leader Flint might change her mind and decide that Midge was too small to be a Dream Fetcher after all.

By the time Team Leader Flint moved on, Midge's ankles had begun to wobble. She settled back onto her heels with a sigh of relief. Next to Midge, Snaffle stood to attention with a smug smile. His uniform had been made by the best tailor in Dreamside. He knew he looked good. *Not like some*, he thought, giving Vert a sideways look. Anyone could see that Vert's uniform was second-hand. It was too tight for him. The material was all washed out and faded. There was a line of darker bands down one sleeve where previous trainees had worn their mission stripes. Snaffle sneered at Vert's uniform.

"Eyes front!" snapped Team Leader Flint. Snaffle jumped and stopped giving Vert sideways looks.

Last in line was Harley, who somehow managed to look relaxed even when she was standing to attention. The truth was, Harley was more than relaxed. She was bored. Spotless uniforms and perfectly polished boots did not interest her. Harley lived to fly. She could hardly wait to jump onto her dreamskoot and head off on her next mission. But first there had to be the inspection. Harley swallowed a yawn and waited for Team Leader Flint to finish. She knew her uniform would pass the inspection. Everything was as it should be, apart from the tattered kerchief that she always wore cowboy-style around her neck. Harley's neckerchief was against regulations, but no one, not even Team Leader Flint, would tell her to take it off. It had once belonged to her mother, and Harley wore it with pride. Her parents were heroes. They had died fighting in the Battle of the Gateway when Harley was only a baby.

"Listen up, Dream Team," said Team Leader Flint, stepping back so that she could glare at all four of them at once. "Your mission today is to deliver dreams to humans in hard-to-find locations. The switchboard room is checking all incoming dream orders right now. They will be picking out four of the more … unusual … deliveries for you. This mission will be a real test of your navigational skills. Once you are Earthside, you must make full use of your tracker maps and your D.R.E.A.M. screens. Understood?"

"Yes, boss," they chorused.

"Good. Now, a reminder about the Three Abiding Rules." Team Leader Flint pointed above the launch pads, where the Three Abiding Rules were written in letters of gold.

Team Leader Flint gave them all

1. *Always* deliver what the customer orders

2. *Don't* look inside the BOX

3. *Never* be SEEN

a very hard look. "I know trainees sometimes find it hard to stick to these rules. For instance," she continued, turning to give Midge an extra-hard glare, "it can be difficult to deliver a nightmare – especially if the human is young. But however 'cute' your customer might be, the Abiding Rules must be obeyed or the whole system will break down. So I'm warning you now. If I catch any one of you deliberately breaking an Abiding Rule, you will be dismissed. No excuses. No exceptions. Understood?"

Midge squirmed under Team Leader Flint's icy glare. On her first solo delivery she had dropped a nightmare meant for a young human onto his bedroom carpet. She had told Team Leader Flint it was an accident, but really she had done it on purpose. Team Leader Flint had been furious. She seemed to know what Midge had done even though she could not prove it. Midge had been put through twelve extra hours of dream-drop training and then had been sent out on a second Earthside delivery before she could pass her solo flying test.

Midge still felt bad about lying to Team Leader Flint – and she was determined not to break any more Abiding Rules – but she did not regret dumping her delivery. She knew that most nightmares were meant to be useful as well as unpleasant: they helped customers to sort out their worries or face up to their fears. But that particular nightmare had been nothing but pure nastiness in a box.

"Understood?" repeated Team Leader Flint, still glaring at Midge.

"Yes, boss," whispered Midge.

"Yes, boss," chorused Vert, Snaffle and Harley.

"Very well." Team Leader Flint turned away from Midge, who slumped with relief. "Vert, you'll be flying first."

Vert gave a strangled whimper.

"Is there a problem, Vert?" asked Team Leader Flint, looking at him closely. He had suddenly gone as pale as uncooked dream-dough.

"No, boss," quavered Vert. He was lying, of course. There was a problem. A very big problem. On his first day of training, Vert had discovered that he was terrified of flying a

dreamskoot. So far he had managed to keep it a secret. He knew how sad his parents would be if he failed his training. They had sacrificed a lot to get him this far – and they were so proud of their son, the trainee Dream Fetcher. Vert would much rather be a Dream Chef than a Dream Fetcher, but he did not have the heart to tell them that.

Team Leader Flint was still staring at him. "Vert? Are you ready for this mission?"

"Yes, boss," said Vert with only a slight wobble to his voice.

"Very well. For these deliveries, you will each take another member of your dream team along with you. Your passenger will be there to watch and learn. They must not help in any way – unless you are in real trouble."

Vert felt his heart lift a little. With

Midge or Harley sitting behind him on the dreamskoot, he might not feel quite so scared.

"Snaffle," said Team Leader Flint. "You will go withVert."

"But—" said Snaffle and Vert, both at the same time.

"No buts," snapped Team Leader Flint.

*Beep, beep, beep.*

Team Leader Flint plucked her pager from her belt and looked at the screen. "The first dream is ready for delivery. To your launch pad, Vert," she ordered. "It's showtime!"

# All at Sea

"**A what?**" squeaked
Vert, climbing very carefully onto his
dreamskoot to make sure it didn't wobble.

"A yacht," said Team Leader Flint.
"You'll be delivering to a human on a
yacht."

"A yacht?" repeated Vert, settling into
the saddle.

"It's a boat with sails," explained
Midge helpfully.

"I know what it is," said Vert. "But how do I find it in all that sea?"

"Just keep heading for the red dot on your tracker map," said Team Leader Flint.

A junior Dream Chef scurried onto the launch pad carrying a freshly baked dream in a flat cardboard box. "There you go, Vert," she said, slotting the box into the padded dream holder on the back of his dreamskoot. "Nice and hot." The Dream Chef hurried away again, lifting her apron to mop her face before plunging back into the steamy kitchens. Vert wished he could follow her.

"Have fun!" said Harley, handing Vert his helmet.

Vert gave Harley a weak smile and began to pull his helmet on. He was just easing it over the points of his ears when Snaffle vaulted into the saddle behind him. The dreamskoot dipped and shook violently. Vert nearly fell off. With a yelp, he jammed his helmet the rest of the way down and grabbed at the handlebars of his dreamskoot to steady himself. Over the hammering of his heart, Vert thought he heard Snaffle snigger. He turned around and frowned into Snaffle's grey, almond-shaped eyes. Snaffle stared back with a look of puzzled innocence.

"Clear the launch pad," ordered Team Leader Flint, striding towards the walkway.

"Good luck, Vert!" called Midge and

Harley, hurrying away after her.

Once the launch pad was clear, Vert gripped his handlebars and gave the first of the take-off commands. "Lift off!"

The anchor ropes fell away and his dreamskoot hummed into life. As it lifted into the air, Vert felt as though he had left his stomach sitting on the launch pad.

"W-wings out," he quavered.

A silvery wing fanned out to either side from beneath the footplates. The dreamskoot hovered, waiting for the final command. Vert felt his throat close up with fear. He could not speak.

"What are you hanging around for?" said Snaffle's voice in the earpiece of his dreamcom.

Vert took a deep breath. "Earthside!" he ordered, opening the throttle.

His dreamskoot shot towards the huge

circular steel
frame that was set into the far wall of
the Dream Centre. This was the gateway
between Dreamside and Earthside. A
skin was stretched across the frame,
full of changing colours. It looked
like water, but it was much thicker. As
his dreamskoot rose up towards the

gateway, Vert closed his eyes and let the Dream Traffic Control autopilot system take control. He still had his eyes closed when his dreamskoot flew into the gateway, but he could tell they were passing through. His whole body felt as though it had been dunked into a bath of warm jelly. The jelly sucked at him for a moment, then let him go again. The temperature dropped as they flew out of the gateway and into the cold night air of Earthside.

Vert felt a small jolt as the Dream Centre autopilot system switched off. It was up to him to fly his dreamskoot now. He forced his eyes open and stared at the two green-lit screens on his control panel. The Earthtown was spread out below him, twinkling with lights, but Vert knew he must not look down. The only way to get through this was to keep his eyes on his navigation screens and pretend he was not flying high above the ground on thin silvery wings.

His tracker map showed three dots. The green dot was his dreamskoot, the blue dot was the gateway behind him and the red dot in the far corner of the screen marked the position of the yacht.

Vert nearly whimpered when he saw how far he had to fly, but then he remembered the dreamcom in his helmet. Snaffle would be able to hear every sound he made. Vert swallowed the whimper and turned his dreamskoot towards the sea.

"Snaffle, I'm heading for the yacht now," he said, into his dreamcom.

"Are you sure you're going the right way?" asked Snaffle, in a worried tone.

"I – I think so," said Vert. "Why?"

"Oh, nothing. I'm sure you know what

you're doing," said Snaffle.

Vert frowned and double-checked his screens. Behind him, Snaffle smiled. He was going to enjoy this flight. When Team Leader Flint had made him go as Vert's passenger, he had been insulted. She had told him to watch and learn, but what could Vert possibly teach him? He, Snaffle, was the best trainee in their dream team. Unfortunately, after his disastrous first mission, Snaffle was sharing third place with Midge. Harley was in second place and, unbelievably, Vert was in the lead. Snaffle scowled briefly at the thought but then his smile returned. If his plan worked, Vert would not be in first place for much longer.

Vert did not need to look down to know he had left the coast and was flying over the sea. The air was colder and he could taste the salt in it. He checked his position on the tracker map and altered his direction slightly. Next he checked his D.R.E.A.M. The D.R.E.A.M. was a radar device in the nose of his dreamskoot that was linked to a screen on the control panel. The letters stood for Danger Recognition and Early Avoidance Monitor. If there were any large, solid objects in his flight path, they would show up as green blobs on the screen. There were no green blobs. His flight path was completely clear. Vert began to feel a bit less frightened. His stomach stopped trying to turn inside out and his shoulders relaxed a little.

"Vert! Look out!" yelled Snaffle, thumping him in the back.

Vert nearly jumped out of the saddle. "Who – what?"

"Down there!" yelled Snaffle, pointing.

"Isn't that the yacht?"

Vert made the mistake of looking where Snaffle was pointing. He saw a fishing trawler bobbing up and down on the moonlit sea. Vert whimpered. It was such a long way down! His head began to spin. His stomach began to lurch. He closed his eyes and kept his mouth firmly shut while he waited for the sick, dizzy feeling to go away.

"Where are you going, Vert?" demanded Snaffle, thumping him again.

Vert opened his eyes and stared at his control panel. He had drifted off course. Grimly, he turned his dreamskoot so that it was once again heading towards the red dot on his tracker screen.

"But you've missed the yacht!" said Snaffle. "It's back there."

"That wasn't the yacht," said Vert,

refusing to look away from his screens.

After that, Snaffle pointed out every ship and boat he could find. He even pointed out an oil rig. "Look!" he would shout, digging his finger into Vert's back. "Isn't that the yacht?"

But Vert would not look down again. He kept his eyes firmly on his navigation screens and tried to ignore Snaffle. Finally the green and red dots on his tracker map moved together. He must be directly above his customer. Vert brought his dreamskoot to a halt and risked one quick downwards glance. A smart little yacht floated on the sea right underneath him.

With a sigh of relief, Vert let his dreamskoot sink down onto the deck. Once there was a solid surface beneath him, Vert could look around without feeling sick or dizzy. Quickly he

checked for any humans or pets. The
deck was quiet and empty. He pressed a
button on the side of his helmet. There
was a tiny hiss and his visor lifted. As
Vert breathed in the fresh night air, he
spotted a set of narrow steps leading
from the deck into the cabin below.

"Do you think the human's down
there?" whispered Vert, pointing to the
steps.

Snaffle lifted his visor too. "I'm not

allowed to help," he said sulkily.

"But – you've been trying to help me all the way here, haven't you?" said Vert.

"Is that what you thought?" sneered Snaffle. He had tried his best to make Vert fly off course, but his plan had failed. Now he would have to find another way to make Vert fail his navigation test.

Vert had no idea what Snaffle was talking about. He shrugged and guided his dreamskoot towards the cabin steps.

*Thud. Thud. Thud.*

Vert frowned. The noise was coming from the bottom of the steps. He edged further forward.

*Thud. Thud. Thud.*

Vert peered over the edge of the top step. The cabin below was in darkness. He had just begun to ease his dreamskoot down the steps when something came flying out of the darkness towards him.

*THUD!*

It was the cabin door. It hit the bottom step and shuddered to a stop centimetres from the nose of his dreamskoot.

*Beep! Beep! Beep!*

The swinging door had activated his D.R.E.A.M. alarm. Vert shut off the alarm and took a few deep breaths to calm himself. The door stayed pressed against the step until the yacht tilted the other way. Slowly the door swung back into the cabin.

"Why would the human leave the cabin door banging like that?" said Vert. "That's not normal, is it?"

"I told you," snapped Snaffle. "I'm not supposed –"

"– to help, I know," sighed Vert. There was only one thing to do. He waited until the door slammed into the bottom step again and then he slipped through the opening.

It was not completely dark inside the cabin. Moonlight shone through a porthole and a soft green glow came from the radio and navigation equipment. Vert peered into every corner. The cabin was empty. He flew across to a doorway in the far wall and hovered in the opening. There was a smaller cabin beyond the doorway. It had been built into the bows of the yacht and was shaped like an iron. A bed filled most of the space. Two humans – one male, one female – were lying in the bed with their heads at the wide end and their feet in the narrow part. Vert froze. Were they awake or asleep? He watched them carefully. They did not move. Both asleep, Vert decided.

He hesitated.

Two of them? Which one had ordered the dream? He checked his delivery details and nodded. The male human was his customer.

"Pass me the dream, please, Snaffle," he asked.

"I'm not supposed to help," said Snaffle, folding his arms.

"But you're right next to it – oh, never mind."

Vert twisted round, reached behind Snaffle and hooked the dream box from the holder. He wedged the box between his knees and steered his dreamskoot into the smaller cabin. There was a bad smell in there. Vert frowned and wrinkled his nose.

"Filthy humans!" hissed Snaffle, slamming his helmet visor down over his face.

Vert let the dream box go. *Phut!* It landed on the male human's chest and instantly disappeared.

"Bission accomplished," said Snaffle, talking through his nose. "Dow can we please ged oud of this stinky blace?"

Vert flew towards the doorway but then slowed to a stop. Something was not right with these humans.

"Cub on!" hissed Snaffle.

Vert ignored him. He flew closer to the

humans and hovered above their faces. It was too dark to see much, but he could hear their ragged breathing and feel a feverish heat rising from their bodies. Vert realized what the bad smell was. It was the sour stink of illness. He decided to take a risk. He pressed a button on the control panel of his dreamskoot. His headlight beam blazed out, lighting up the faces of the humans.

"Are you crazy?" whispered Snaffle. "You'll wake them up! Abiding Rule Number Three – *Never be seen!*"

"I don't think they're going to wake up," said Vert, staring down at the humans below him. They were both sweating a lot and their skin had a grey tinge to it. "They're very sick."

"Really?" Snaffle took a look. "Don't get too close."

"I can't just leave them drifting in the

middle of the sea like this," muttered Vert. "Anything could happen. The yacht could sink. They could die."

"What do you care?" asked Snaffle. "You've made your delivery."

Vert flew back into the main cabin and landed on the desk in front of the radio equipment. Climbing from his dreamskoot with a determined look on his face, he walked over to the radio and studied the array of buttons and dials.

"What are you doing?" demanded Snaffle as Vert picked up a pen and rested it across his shoulder like a spear.

Vert marched up to the radio and started pushing buttons with the pen. "I'm – trying – to – get – help –" he panted.

"But they're only humans," said Snaffle. "And you're not supposed to—" He stopped without finishing his

sentence. A slow smile spread across his
face. Why not let Vert do whatever he
wanted? Then, when they got back to
Dreamside, Snaffle could make a very
detailed report to Team Leader Flint.

Vert pressed buttons and prodded dials
until his arms were too tired to hold the
pen. The radio remained stubbornly

silent. He dropped the pen onto the desk and looked around. There must be something else he could use to raise the alarm. He spotted a large orange torch in a wall bracket next to the radio. The letters E.P.I.R.B. were printed on it. Vert climbed back onto his dreamskoot and flew up to the torch.

"*Emergency Position Indicating Radio Beacon*," he read. "Oh! It's not a torch, it's a beacon! If I can work out how to switch this on, it will transmit a distress signal to the human emergency services."

He moved his dreamskoot across to the printed instructions on the wall next to the beacon. "Now, let's see. *To activate automatically, lift from bracket.*" He looked at the beacon. It was nearly three times as big as he was. "Hmm. Perhaps not." Vert went back to the instructions. "*To activate manually, press button on rear of device.* That's more like it."

Vert shone his headlight into the gap behind the beacon. He could see the button. He brought his dreamskoot alongside the bracket. "Halt!" he ordered. The dreamskoot hovered in place. Carefully, Vert slid his bottom out of the saddle and onto the metal bracket. He stood up and edged behind the beacon. Once there, he braced his back against the wall,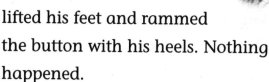 lifted his feet and rammed the button with his heels. Nothing happened.

"Come on!" yelled Vert, pushing as hard as he could. Suddenly, the button clicked inwards.

*Eek ... eek ... eek!*

The beacon began to shriek and send out flashes of light.

"Now you've done it!" shouted Snaffle as Vert scrambled back onto the dreamskoot.

"I hope so!" yelled Vert.

"Go. Now!" ordered Snaffle, glancing warily towards the cabin where the humans were sleeping.

"No," said Vert.

Snaffle stared. Vert never stood up to him. "Pardon?" he said.

"This is my mission," explained Vert. "And those humans are my customers. I'm staying here to make sure help arrives. We can hide somewhere on deck."

As Vert skimmed the deck looking for a hiding place, Snaffle sat back and thought about the terrible report he was going to make to Team Leader Flint when he got home. To his surprise, the idea of getting Vert into trouble did not make him feel very happy. For a few seconds, Snaffle even considered forgetting all about his report. Quickly, he gave himself a very hard pinch. He could not show any weakness now. After his disastrous first mission, Snaffle knew he had no hope of beating his brother Grabble's graduation score, but he could still gain the highest marks in his dream team. That would be enough to make his parents proud of him, wouldn't it? Snaffle scowled at the back of Vert's head. Vert's stupid parents seemed to be proud of him just for being there. What was the point in that?

Vert found a narrow space behind
a foot locker. He folded away his
dreamskoot wings and backed the little
machine into his chosen hiding place.
There he waited, squashed up against
the hull of the yacht with Snaffle hissing
a stream of threats and warnings into
his ear. It seemed like a very long time
before he heard a distant engine.

*Blat-blat-blat-blat—*

"Can you hear that, Snaffle?" said
Vert. "Something's coming."

"Good. Let's go."

Vert listened. The noise was getting
louder. "It doesn't sound like a boat." He
stuck out his head to have a look.

*Blat-blat-blat-BLAT-BLAT—*

Vert pulled his head back in and gave
Snaffle a horrified stare.

"What?" demanded Snaffle.

"Brace yourself."

"What do you mean?"

"BRACE YOURSELF!" bawled Vert, sliding his visor down. "IT'S A HELICOPTER!"

Vert and Snaffle wedged themselves into their hiding place by stretching their arms out sideways and jamming their hands flat against the foot locker and the hull of the yacht. The air began to churn and tug at their clothes. Sand and bits of dried seaweed rose up from the deck and swirled around them. The helicopter's searchlight found the yacht and suddenly it was as bright as day.

*BLAT-BLAT-BLAT-BLAT!*

The noise of the rotor blades made their helmets vibrate. The blast was so strong, it threatened to knock them from the dreamskoot. Vert looked up. An enormous yellow rescue helicopter was hovering overhead. The door on the side

of the helicopter opened and a human was lowered down to the yacht. A pair of huge boots thumped onto the deck right in front of them. The human unclipped himself and disappeared into the cabin. A few minutes later he was back, shouting into his radio mike. "Severe food poisoning…" he yelled. "Emergency … immediate transfer to hospital…"

After that, everything happened very quickly. While Vert and Snaffle cowered behind the locker, another human with a special stretcher was lowered to the deck. Within minutes, the two sick humans had been carried from the cabin and winched up to the helicopter one at a time. Then the helicopter blat-blatted away again, lighting up the sea with its searchlight as it went. The noise stopped. The swirling wind dropped. The yacht returned to rocking gently on the sea.

"Happy now?" said Snaffle.

"Yes, thank you," said Vert. And he was. He might be only seven centimetres high but suddenly Vert felt a lot taller. He had saved two humans and he had not been scared once. For the first time, Vert did not feel like an imposter in his Dream Fetcher uniform.

Back at the Dream Centre, his happiness did not last long. As soon as they were on the ground, Snaffle scurried off to see Team Leader Flint.

"You did it, Vert!" smiled Midge, hurrying onto his launch pad.

Vert nodded absently, gazing after Snaffle.

"Put it there, Ace," said Harley.

Automatically Vert reached out to shake Harley's hand, but she whisked it away at the last second and thumbed her nose at him instead.

"Every time!" crowed Harley. "You fall for it every time!"

Vert did not even smile. Harley and Midge looked at one another and then turned to see what was making Vert so anxious. They spotted Snaffle and Team Leader Flint standing close together on the walkway at the back of the launch pads. Snaffle was talking and waving his arms about. Team Leader

Flint was nodding and making notes on her clipboard. Both of them kept looking over at Vert.

"What's going on?" demanded Harley.

"Snaffle is making a report," said Vert, miserably. "On some things I did in my navigation test."

"You mean Snaffle is telling tales," said Midge quietly.

Over on the walkway, Team Leader Flint gave a final nod and then strode onto the launch pad with Snaffle scurrying along behind her. Vert straightened his shoulders and stood to attention.

"Vert," said Team Leader Flint. "Is it true that you interfered with human radio equipment during your navigation test?"

"Um – a bit."

"And that you deliberately brought

human rescuers to the yacht?"

"I made sure we weren't seen,"
pleaded Vert. "I didn't break any of the
Abiding Rules."

"Is it true?" snapped Team Leader
Flint.

"Yes, boss," sighed Vert.

"Very well. There's only one thing
I can do." Team Leader Flint frowned
down at her clipboard. Vert felt his chin
start to wobble. He realized he was going
to miss being part of this dream team.
Midge and Harley shared a horrified
glance. Even Snaffle stopped smirking.
He had only meant to knock a few
points off Vert's score, not have him
dismissed.

Finally, Team Leader Flint looked
up again. They all held their breath.
"Trainee Vert," she said. "What you did
today was risky and beyond the call of

duty. Your brave actions saved two humans. That's what I call good customer care."

Vert blinked. "Excuse me?" he said.

"Oh, do listen!" snapped Team Leader Flint. "Without your quick thinking and bravery we would have lost two valued customers. Trainee Vert, I'm awarding you fifty bonus points."

# Pure Wonder

**Harley** flew across the night sky above a swaying line of trucks and caravans. The truck headlights lit up the dark road beneath her dreamskoot. They were pointing the way to a field on the edge of an Earthside town. Excitement fizzed up Harley's spine and tingled in the roots of her hair as she gazed at the field.

"We found it, Midge!" she yelled into her dreamcom. "We found the circus!"

Midge was riding behind Harley. "No, *you* found it," she said. "I'm only the passenger." She gave Harley a quick hug. "Well done."

"What for?"

"Tracking the caravan. It's hard to follow a moving target."

"Oh, that. Easy peasy," said Harley, carelessly. "Look at it, though," she sighed, gazing down at the field. "A circus!"

Harley thought most humans were deadly dull creatures, but circus people were different. She had learned all about them in Human Studies. They were adventurers and risk-takers, just like her. Harley had always wanted to see some circus people for herself. Now she had her chance. Her navigation test was to deliver a dream to a customer in a travelling circus.

In one corner of the circus field, a caravan village had sprung up on the grass. There were more caravans rolling in from the road all the time, including the one Harley had been tracking. A little girl called Maria was fast asleep inside, waiting for her dream order to arrive. Harley looked down at the gently glowing windows of the caravan village and then gazed across at the brighter lights in the middle of the field. The brightest light of all was coming from the biggest tent she had ever seen. The Big Top. Hundreds of humans were hurrying across the grass towards it. A circus band was playing inside. The show was about to begin!

"Where are you going?" asked Midge into Harley's dreamcom. "You have a navigation test to pass, remember?"

Harley jumped. She had been drifting towards the bright Big Top like a moth to a light bulb. She shook herself and turned back. Maria's caravan was parked up now. The truck that had been towing it was gone. Everything seemed quiet. Harley darted down to the caravan and skooted around the outside, checking the windows.

"Bingo," she said softly, peering in through a gap in the curtains of one window. "Maria's bedroom."

Harley flew up to the caravan roof and spotted an open fanlight. "I'm going in," she whispered, steering her dreamskoot through the gap. Once inside, Harley hovered just below the ceiling while she checked out the tiny bedroom. No pets. No other humans. The only noise was the *chug-chug-chug* of the generator

outside. Maria was curled up in a bed so
full of pillows and soft toys that it was
difficult to see her.

"Ahh," said Midge, looking down at
the little human girl. "Isn't she sweet?"

Harley rolled her eyes. "Dream box,
please."

Midge passed the box over. Harley
swooped down and dropped the dream
neatly onto Maria's cheek. *Phut!* The

dream disappeared. Harley turned her dreamskoot and heard Midge give a gasp of horror. She looked up. Someone was opening the bedroom door! Harley stopped dead. She had heard nothing over the constant chugging of the caravan generator and now there was no time to escape. Harley did the only thing left to do. She drove her dreamskoot into the middle of the pile of soft toys on Maria's bed and then pressed the shut-down button.

The dreamskoot sighed into silence and came to rest at the head of a large teddy bear, just as a human female stepped into the bedroom. Harley and Midge froze. The dreamskoot was completely hidden, but their heads and shoulders were sticking up out of the tangled mess of soft toys. Surely they would be spotted?

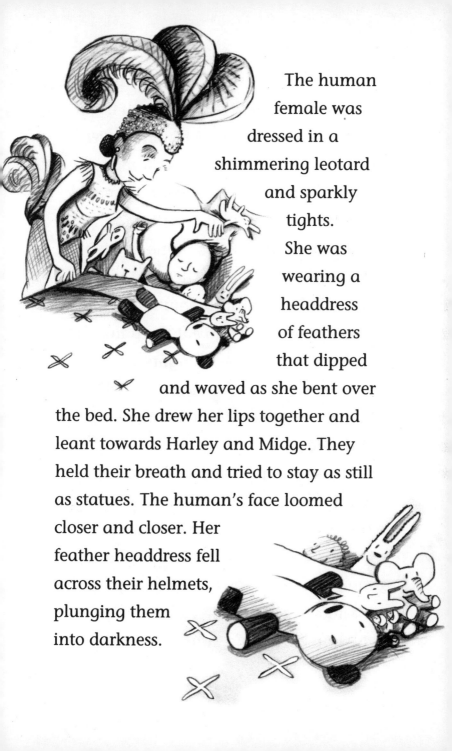

The human female was dressed in a shimmering leotard and sparkly tights. She was wearing a headdress of feathers that dipped and waved as she bent over the bed. She drew her lips together and leant towards Harley and Midge. They held their breath and tried to stay as still as statues. The human's face loomed closer and closer. Her feather headdress fell across their helmets, plunging them into darkness.

Midge heard the human's lips smacking together and nearly fainted with fright. There was no record of a human ever eating a Dream Fetcher, but Midge supposed there was always a first time.

"Sweet dreams," said the human, straightening up and smiling down at Maria. Midge gave a little gasp of relief as she realized that the human had not been leaning down to eat them up. She had been kissing her daughter.

"I can't believe she didn't see us!" said Midge as soon as the bedroom door closed behind the human.

Harley did not answer. She was staring at a framed poster on the wall above Maria's bed. Her eyes were big and shiny. "Look," she said softly. "Maria's mum is a hero too. Just like my mum."

Midge looked at the poster. It showed the human female in her sparkly costume. She was flying through the air high above the circus ring. Her arms were stretched out towards a human male, who was hanging upside down from a trapeze. He was also wearing a sparkly costume, but his was like a very tight all-in-one sleepsuit. The bright red writing across the top of the poster said:

Privately, Midge did not think the human female was a hero. It was certainly very brave to perform on the high trapeze every night, but being a hero was not just about taking risks. Harley's mum was a hero because she had sacrificed her own life to save others. Midge thought about pointing this out, but Harley was gazing at the poster with a wistful look on her face. Harley's ears were out of sight inside her helmet, but Midge knew they would be drooping a little. She patted Harley on the back. "Let's go home," she said quietly.

"Are you kidding?" said Harley, backing her dreamskoot out of the pile of soft toys. "I have to see the Flying Paninis!"

Midge protested all the way to the Big Top, but Harley wasn't listening. She zipped around the outside of the huge tent until she found a gap in the canvas large enough to slip through.

"Don't go in there!" said Midge. "It's full of humans – and they're all awake!"

"They won't see us. I guarantee it. They'll be too busy watching the show."

"But—"

"Midge, you worry too much," said Harley, easing through the gap. "You're always worrying about something. Lighten up!"

Midge scowled. It was all very well for Harley. If she was dismissed for breaking one of the Three Abiding Rules, she would just stroll off and find something else to do. For Midge it was different. Nothing meant more to her than becoming a Dream Fetcher. If she was thrown out of the training programme, her world would crumble.

They came out at the back of the
ranks of stadium seating. Harley
dodged through the tangle of ropes and
scaffolding until she was directly under
the front row of seats. She found a spot
where there were no human feet to block
their view of the circus ring. "Best seats
in the house," she grinned, parking her
dreamskoot on a handy metal strut.

Harley lifted her
visor and settled back in the saddle.

Midge sat rigidly, listening to the
shuffling of human feet and the rumble
of human voices all around her. She
had never been this close to so many
humans at once. A fanfare of trumpets
blasted out, signalling the start of the
show. The ringmaster marched in at
the head of a circus parade and the
audience applauded and stamped their
feet. Underneath the seats the noise was
deafening! Slowly, Midge realized that
Harley was right. The humans were too

interested in what was happening in the ring to notice them. She lifted her visor, breathed in the smell of fresh sawdust and began to watch the show.

There were spindly-legged stilt walkers, tumbling acrobats, posturing fire eaters and rowdy gangs of clowns. Midge was enthralled, but Harley was growing more and more impatient. She kept glancing up into the roof of the Big Top. Finally, the moment arrived. Maria's mother and the male human walked into the centre of the ring, hand in hand. They stood very straight in their sparkly costumes as the ringmaster introduced them.

"Ladies and Gentlemen, we are proud to present, all the way from Italy, the most daring trapeze act in the world. The Flying Paninis!"

The audience applauded and the

Flying Paninis bowed. Two thin rope-ladders unfurled from the roof, one on each side of the ring. The Flying Paninis each took hold of a ladder. A drum roll rumbled like thunder. Together, they began to climb the swaying ladders. Higher and higher they climbed with fast, steady steps. Soon they were higher than a house. The audience gazed up at the two humans caught in the spotlight. Still they climbed upwards, hand over hand, their costumes sparkling in the lights.

More spotlights came on, lighting up the whole of the roofspace. Finally, the audience could see what the Flying Paninis were climbing towards. Two trapezes hung from slender threads right in the highest part of the roof.

"Ohhhh," sighed the audience, all together.

"Oh!" said Harley, a second later. She stopped watching the Flying Paninis and began going through her pockets instead.

"What are you looking for?" asked Midge.

"Aha! Here it is," said Harley, holding up a tiny black box.

"What's that?" asked Midge.

"This is a signalling device," said Harley. She unooked a thin silver aerial from one corner of the box.

"What are you doing with that?" squeaked Midge.

"I'm sending a signal, of course." Harley pressed a button on the box. A green light began to flash. "There. He should be arriving any minute now."

"Who should?" asked Midge anxiously, peering into the dark corners under the seating.

"A friend of mine," said Harley. "He's called Dare."

Midge was getting more worried by the second. "But – but why is he coming here?"

"Did you hear all the humans go *Ohhh* just now?"

"Ye-es."

"And the Flying Paninis aren't even on the trapeze yet!" laughed Harley. "Can you imagine what will happen once they start their act?"

"What?" asked Midge.

"There's going to be a huge burst of Pure Wonder from the audience, that's what! And you know what a rare ingredient Pure Wonder is. The Dream Chefs are always on the lookout for it. Dare wouldn't want to miss this chance to collect some."

"So your friend Dare is a ... Collector?"

Midge shuddered as she said the word. Collectors supplied the Dream Kitchens with raw dream ingredients. They were a vital part of dream production, but Midge could not help being a bit frightened of them. Collectors and their families lived deep underground in The Below. Long ago, Collectors had moved freely between the surface and The Below, but slowly they had come to prefer the dark. Now The Below was their home as well as their workplace and Collectors were rarely seen on the surface of Dreamside.

There was an underground gateway in The Below which allowed Collectors to pass through to Earthside. There they worked in a sprawling network of underground tunnels just big enough for their collecting carts to trundle back and forth. Every now and then, the tunnels opened out into a collecting cavern. The location of every cavern had been chosen very carefully. Each one had been hollowed out under an Earthside place where waking humans gathered to share strong feelings. There were collection caverns under theatres and cinemas, churches and football stadiums, hospitals and airports.

The human feelings from these places seeped down into the earth and were filtered through collecting pipes, which had been drilled into the cavern roof. The distilled feelings dripped from the end of the pipes into the carts below. When a goal was scored, the Collectors gathered every roar of excitement and every groan of misery. When a human baby was born, the Collectors stored each second of newness and every tear of joy. Each airport "hello" and

"goodbye" was collected too – and every heartfelt human prayer.

The Collectors carried the human feelings back to Dreamside in their carts. There, they were sorted, graded and sent up to the Dream Kitchens. The rare feelings, such as Pure Wonder and Golden Grace, were sold for a high price. Other feelings, such as envy, anger and spite, were much cheaper because they were as common as weeds. Nothing went to waste, though. The Collectors sent all leftover human feelings to the Dreamside power plants, where they were put to

good use as fuel. The energy sucked from Earthside road rage and human toddler tantrums lit up Dreamside homes, heated Dream Kitchen ovens and powered dreamskoots.

During their basic training, Midge, Harley, Vert and Snaffle had been taken far beneath the Dream Centre to see for themselves how the Collectors lived and worked. The elevator ride down to The Below had taken a very long time. When the doors finally opened, they had stepped out into deep twilight. They had been allowed to use their helmet lamps only on the dimmest setting, but even that small amount of extra light was too much for the Collectors. The special guides who came forward to greet them had to wear thick wraparound shades to protect their eyes. Their skin was mushroom-white and damp to the touch.

Now Midge shuddered again as she remembered the clammy handshake of the Collector guide. "Is he –?" she asked, her eyes darting between Harley and the darker corners under the Big Top seats. "– is Dare a Collector?"

"No. Dare lives above ground. He's not a Collector." Harley gave Midge a sideways look. "But he does collect."

Midge's eyes widened. "He's a Maverick!" she gasped. "But that's wrong!"

Mavericks made a living by tracking down and collecting sudden or unexpected outbursts of human feeling. They worked for themselves and were frowned upon by some in Dreamside.

"What's wrong about it?" challenged Harley.

"He takes work away from the Collectors," said Midge.

"No, he doesn't. He works above ground, finding places like this, where there are no collecting caverns."

"Well, there you are, then. Working above ground without back-up," said Midge. "What if he's seen? Mavericks put us all at risk."

Harley grinned. "You worry too much," she said fondly.

A burst of applause from the circus audience made Harley turn back to the ring. The Flying Paninis had reached their trapezes and were starting to swing higher and higher. "He's going to miss this if he doesn't hurry," she muttered.

"Miss what?" asked Dare, suddenly appearing beside them with a swish of dreamskoot wings.

"Hey! You made it!" Harley reached over to give Dare a hug. "Midge, meet my friend Dare. He lost his parents in the Battle of the Gateway too. We grew up together in the orphanage."

Midge studied Dare. His dreamskoot was battered and dirty, but the engine purred with energy. So did Dare. Every bit of him seemed to be full of life. His blue eyes sparkled and his hair was wild and spiky. Dare grinned and stuck out his hand. Midge scowled and folded her arms.

"You should be wearing a helmet," she said. "It's dangerous to ride without one."

"Nice to meet you too, Midge," said Dare, withdrawing his hand.

"She's a bit of a worrier," said Harley.

"Oh," said Dare, as though that explained everything. Midge's scowl deepened.

"So. Thanks for the tip-off. What do we have here?" asked Dare.

"Pure Wonder," said Harley. "Any minute now."

An extra-loud drum roll came from the circus band. "Ladies and Gentlemen!" boomed the ringmaster. "I must ask for complete silence as the amazing Flying Paninis prepare to perform one of the most difficult catches ever attempted."

Dare opened a box on the back of his dreamskoot. "Want to help?" he asked.

"Yeah!" grinned Harley.

"No!" said Midge. "We can't go out there, Harley!"

"I'll keep you safe," said Harley. "Promise."

"We just can't!" squeaked Midge. "What if we're seen?"

Harley looked at Midge and saw the fear in her eyes. "OK," she said gently. "We won't. But you shouldn't worry so much, Midge. After all…" Harley turned to Dare. They shared a sad smile and finished the sentence together. "What's the worst that can happen?"

Suddenly Midge felt ashamed. For Harley and Dare, the worst had already happened. Their parents were dead. Midge stared up at the Flying Paninis. They were each hanging upside down with their legs hooked over their trapeze bars. The audience was so quiet, Midge could hear the faint creak of the ropes as they swung together – and apart. Together – and apart. Their timing had to be perfect for this catch.

Midge looked back to Harley. The Flying Paninis trusted one another with their lives. Surely she could trust Harley to keep her safe? She took a deep breath. "Can I change my mind?" she said in a small voice.

Dare winked at Midge and pulled three tightly packed bundles of metal rods from the box on the back of his dreamskoot. He handed one each to Harley and Midge and kept the third for himself. They pressed the buttons on the side of the bundles. The metal rods sprang apart, unfolding into three long-handled nets.

"And you'll need these," said Dare, handing them each a pair of green-tinted shades. "To see what you're collecting."

Harley and Midge put on their shades through the front of their helmets. "Let's go," said Harley.

Midge put her arms around Harley's waist. Dare and Harley turned their dreamskoots away from the ring and flew under the seating until they reached the tent wall. They pointed their dreamskoots upwards and began to climb together, skimming the canvas all the way. Their dreamskoots shot out from behind the top row of seats just as a huge gasp burst from the audience. In the roof-space of the Big Top, Maria's mother had let go of her trapeze. She flew through the air, somersaulting over and over in the spotlights. She was spinning so fast, her glittery costume seemed to give off sparks.

The audience gasped again. Harley and Midge looked down at the upturned human faces through their green-tinted shades. Suddenly there were sparks everywhere. Bright fragments of Pure Wonder were flying from the open mouths of the audience and twisting upwards like thousands of fireflies.

"Now!" yelled Dare.

Harley peeled off to the right. Dare peeled off to the left. They swooped over the heads of the audience, holding out their nets to catch the twirling flecks of Pure Wonder. Not one human spotted them. Everyone was watching the spinning woman tumble towards the outstretched hands of her partner. Would he catch her before she tumbled too far? He stretched out his arms, but there was still a gap. The audience gasped again. He was going to miss! Then at the last second the spinning woman unfolded. She arched her back and stretched out her arms. Her partner grabbed her by the wrists and held on tight.

The audience rose to their feet with a roar. They clapped their hands and stamped their feet. Harley did a loop-the-loop in honour of the human who reminded her of her own mother. Even Midge forgot to worry for a while. She laughed with the excitement of it as she leant out over the audience, filling her net to the top with sparks of Pure Wonder.

"Time to go," said Dare, zooming up beside them.

The audience were still on their feet applauding the Flying Paninis. "Just a bit longer," pleaded Midge.

"Listen to you!" laughed Harley. "But we have to go. The humans are going to start looking around and noticing other things – including us – any minute now."

Harley and Midge followed Dare out through a gap in the tent wall. Together, they zipped across the circus field and soared up into the dark Earthside sky like tiny comets, leaving a sparkling trail of Pure Wonder behind them.

# Remembrance

"Oh dear.
Oh dear me. Oops-a-daisy.
Oh my! Oh, dear me."

"Vert," sighed Midge. "You're doing it again."

"Sorry," said Vert.

Midge smiled to herself. Sharing a dreamskoot with Vert was very different from sharing a dreamskoot with Harley. And she should know. She had barely climbed off Harley's dreamskoot when she had been sent Earthside again on her own navigation test, with Vert as her passenger.

"Midge, you'll be delivering a dream to a customer in hospital," Team Leader Flint had said. "Finding the hospital will be no problem. Finding the correct bed without being seen is a different story. That is your navigation challenge."

Team Leader Flint had been right. The hospital had been easy to find. Midge had not even needed her navigation screens. She had simply headed for the glass and concrete block on the edge of the Earthside town. It was hard to miss. There were lights all over the outside of the building, from the ambulance bay on the ground floor to the helicopter pad on the roof.

It had also been easy to find a way in. Midge had slipped quietly through the loading bay doors at the back of the hospital without any fuss. But now the easy part was over. Midge had to find one old man in a hospital filled with at least five hundred beds. She eased her dreamskoot through a doorway at the back of the loading bay and came out into a long corridor. Quickly, she zipped up to the ceiling and hovered there while she checked out the corridor. It was the middle of the night Earthside, but Midge knew there would always be waking humans in a hospital, whatever the time. The corridor was empty. Midge let out her breath and took a closer look around. The corridor was lit with bare bulbs and the breeze-block walls were unpainted.

"This doesn't look like the bit where they keep the patients," she whispered into her dreamcom. "We need to go higher."

"Higher?" quavered Vert, clamping his arms more firmly around her waist.

"I think so." Midge pressed a button on her control panel, and a three-dimensional map of the hospital came up on her tracker screen. The green dot in the basement was her dreamskoot. The red dot on the third floor was her customer. "There he is. We want the third floor. I'm going to find a way up."

"O-OK."

There were double swing doors at each end of the corridor. At one end, the doors were propped open. Steam was drifting out into the corridor and Midge could hear human voices. She turned her dreamskoot and headed for the other end of the corridor, dodging between high-sided metal trolleys stacked with tins of tomatoes and sacks of flour.

"Oh dear. Oh, my. Oops-a-daisy," said

Vert with every swerve of the
dreamskoot.

Midge braked. Her dreamskoot came
to a halt and hovered in mid-air.

"I'm doing it again, aren't I," said Vert
in a small voice.

"Yep," said Midge. "You don't need to
worry, Vert. I'm not as good as Harley,
but I can handle a dreamskoot. We'll be
fine."

"Sorry. I'll try to stop."

Midge reached the other end of the
corridor and hovered outside a round
window in the top of the door. Beyond
the glass she could see the hospital
kitchens. They were quiet and dark.
Midge pushed the nose of her
dreamskoot against one of the swing
doors. The little machine whined with
effort, but the door would not move.

"Too heavy," muttered Midge. "We'll

have to see what's through those other doors."

"Be careful," whispered Vert. "There are humans in there."

Midge flew back to the far end of the corridor and peered into the steamy room. Just inside the doors, a huge and complicated machine was pressing and folding bed sheets at high speed. The steam was coming from the machine. At the other end of the room, two yawning humans were pulling another load of sheets from a row of enormous washing machines.

"It's a – what do you call it?" whispered Midge.

"A laundry," said Vert.

Midge spotted a square hole in the wall, halfway between the pressing machine and the humans. The trolley below the hole was full of dirty laundry.

Midge smiled. "Look," she said, pointing to the hole in the wall.

"That's a laundry chute," said Vert.

"It's also our way up to the third floor," said Midge.

She checked the humans again. They both had their backs turned. Midge eased in through the open doors and made her way across the room, dodging from one hiding place to another until she reached the laundry chute and disappeared inside.

"That went well," she said, turning to give Vert a smile as her dreamskoot rose up inside the metal chute.

"Look out!" cried Vert.

Midge looked up. A ball of dirty sheets was tumbling down the chute towards them. With a gasp, Midge turned her dreamskoot around and shot back out into the laundry room just ahead of the sheets.

"Look out!" yelled Vert again.

Midge let out a scream. One of the humans was trundling his trolley across the room towards the pressing machine – and she was flying straight towards his head.

Midge yanked her dreamskoot over to the left so hard, the engine nearly stalled.

"Please … please … please…" she whispered as the little machine floundered to a halt. After what seemed like hours, the engine stuttered back into life and the dreamskoot

began to move again. Midge zipped away, skimming so close to the human's head that his hair lifted in the breeze of her passing. The human put a hand to his forehead and looked around with a puzzled frown. Quickly, Midge dodged through the pressing machine.

"Look out!" yelled Vert for the third time.

Midge shot out of the machine just as a huge metal press slammed down behind her with a loud hiss. A burst of steam blasted from the press and breathed hotly down their necks as they skidded across the laundry floor. Their dreamskoot came to a stop under the front wheels of the trolley. At that moment, the human started walking again.

"Midge!" squealed Vert as the trolley wheels rumbled heavily across the concrete towards them.

Midge opened the throttle and put on a desperate burst of speed. She nearly made it, but the trolley wheel grazed the back of her dreamskoot and sent them spinning towards the wall. Midge braked and pulled up on the handlebars as hard as she could. Her dreamskoot shot up the wall – and back into the laundry chute.

Midge closed her eyes as the dreamskoot rode smoothly up the metal tube to the third floor. She was shaking all over.

"Oh, my," breathed Vert. "We were nearly rolled up in a dirty sheet. Then we were nearly ironed flat. Then we were nearly steamed. Then we were nearly squished. Oh dear. Oh, my. Oh dear me."

"Vert," sighed Midge.

"Sorry."

The third-floor corridor had lights with pretty shades. There were paintings on the walls and coloured tiles on the floor. "This looks more like it," whispered Midge, easing her dreamskoot out of the laundry chute.

The corridor was empty but Midge floated up to the ceiling just in case. Humans hardly ever looked above their heads. It was scary to be out in the open but there were plenty of side corridors to zip into if a human should appear. Midge decided to risk it. She checked the red dot on her tracker screen. "Dead ahead," she said, setting off.

"Oh, my," breathed Vert, trying to look everywhere at once. "Oh dear. Dear me..."

Midge cruised along just below the ceiling, reading all the signs. "Here we are. Ward Thirty-two." She turned her dreamskoot down a side corridor. First they came to a small room where two humans in uniforms sat behind a high desk. One was reading and the other was knitting. Midge brought her dreamskoot down below desk level and sneaked past the humans into a long room with all the lights turned off.

In the light that shone in from the doorway, Midge counted twenty beds, ten down each side of the ward. In every bed a human male lay sleeping. Which one was her customer? Midge checked the name on her delivery details and then cruised down the middle of the ward, reading the names at the bottom of the beds.

"This is him," she said, stopping at the very last bed on the left-hand side. "William Shaw." A thin old man lay on

his back, propped up with pillows. He
was very still. His breathing was shallow.
A heart monitor beeped beside the bed.
"Pass me the dream box," said Midge.

"William Shaw. I know that name,"
said Vert, handing the dream box
to Midge and then leaning over her
shoulder to peer curiously at the sleeping
human. "He's a bit of a
legend in the Dream
Kitchens – one of

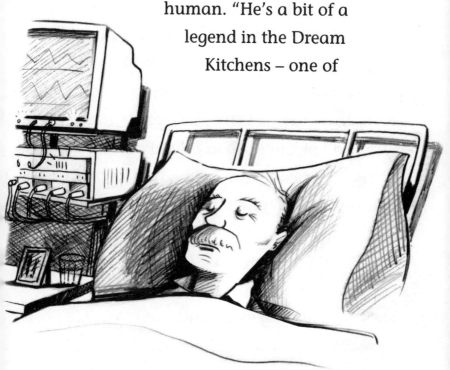

their best customers. He's been placing dream orders with us every night for eighty years."

"Eighty years? Really?" said Midge. She stared down at the thin old man in the bed. He did not look the sort to have a big dream appetite. "What kind of dreams?"

"Oh, the usual selection. But for the past sixty-three years there's been one dream he's kept ordering more than any other," said Vert. "Sometimes he'll have two or three of those in one night. Motza, the Head Dream Chef, let me make one once. He said I did a good job." Vert could not help a note of pride creeping into his voice. He loved making dreams.

"What did you make?" asked Midge.

"A guilt dream," said Vert. "Something about running away and leaving someone behind."

"Oh." Midge looked down at the dream box in her hand. Suddenly she did not feel so good about her delivery. Sixty-three years. That was a long time to feel guilty. Midge shook herself and did a quick safety check around the bed.

First she looked for her escape route. The window above William's bedside cupboard was open. Midge flew up to the window to check the gap. She nodded happily. The gap was big enough.

There was nothing under the bed. The top of William's bedside cupboard was nearly empty too. All the other patients had get-well cards and bunches of flowers and family photographs. William only had one framed photograph on display. Midge went in to have a look. The photograph behind the glass was old and creased and going brown at the edges. It showed two young men in army uniform.

Their shirts were open. Their sleeves were rolled up. They were laughing into the camera and they had their arms draped across one another's shoulders. Midge looked more closely. The dark-haired soldier was a much younger William Shaw. Midge wondered whether the fair-haired young man next to William was the one he still felt so guilty about.

"Midge? Are you OK?"

Midge shook herself again. "Sorry, Vert. I'm going in for the drop."

She flew over the bed and dropped the dream onto William's chest.

*Phut!* The dream disappeared. Midge flew up to the window. She was about to slip through the gap when she heard a groan behind her. She looked back. William's face had creased up in sorrow. "I'm sorry," he groaned in his sleep. "I'm so sorry, James. I didn't mean to." As Midge and Vert watched, a tear trickled from William's eye and slid down his cheek.

"Sixty-three years?" said Midge, once they were safely out of the hospital and flying back to the gateway. "He's been ordering that dream for sixty-three years?"

"Yes," gulped Vert.

"Right," said Midge firmly. "Something has to be done."

"But what can we do?" asked Vert.

"Did you say he sometimes orders two or three guilt dreams a night?"

"Yes," said Vert. "Especially when he hasn't had one for a few weeks."

"Hmm," said Midge. "I think I might have a plan."

"Hey!" shouted Motza, across the Dream Kitchens. "It's-a my little friend Vert! And who is the lovely lady you bring to see me?" Motza strode across the kitchens towards Vert and Midge, wiping his red face on his apron.

"This is Midge," said Vert. "She wants to see inside the Dream Kitchens. Can I show her around?"

Motza's big face grew serious. He bent down to look into their eyes. "Have you finished your deliveries for this shift?" he said. Vert knew why Motza was asking. One of the Abiding Rules for a Dream Fetcher was, *Don't look inside the box.* Motza wanted to be sure that Vert and Midge would not accidentally catch sight of a dream they might be delivering later on.

"Yes," said Vert, truthfully. "We're

finished for the night. We both just passed our navigation tests."

"Hey! That's-a my boy!" Motza beamed. "And well done to you too, Midge. Go ahead," he added, as he hurried away to check an oven. "Look around. But keep out of the way of my chefs!"

Vert took Midge over to the counter at the front of the Dream Kitchens. Above the counter, hundreds of squares of white paper were hanging from little metal clips. "Incoming dream orders," muttered Vert, pointing to the paper squares. "If there's another one from William Shaw, it'll be here. Just look for his name."

Together they moved along the row of orders, reading names. Dream Chefs were running up all the time, snatching a slip from the end of the row and rushing away to prepare the order. Midge began to get worried. If William had placed a second order, what if it was snatched away before they could get to it?

"Here it is!" cried Vert. He reached up and yanked William's dream order off the clip just before the next chef appeared to grab it. "It's another guilt dream. Come on. Follow me."

Vert moved through the kitchens,

pointing everything out to Midge as though giving her a tour. At the same time, he was quietly choosing raw dream toppings and slipping them into the helmet that Midge carried in the crook of her arm.

"Got everything?" asked Midge as they reached a quiet corner at the back of the kitchens.

"I think so," said Vert. He rolled out a spare piece of dream-dough and then picked his way through the toppings in Midge's helmet, muttering away to himself as he arranged them on the dough. Finally, he gave a satisfied nod and slipped the dream into the back of a spare oven. A few minutes later, it was ready.

"I wish we could see how it works," said Midge as Vert plucked an empty dream box from the top of a stack.

"Oh!" said Vert. "Hang on. I've just had an idea." He put back the box he had picked up and searched through the stack until he found the one he wanted. "Look," he said, pointing to a small tag clipped to the box. "See that? It's a quality-control tag."

"Clever," said Midge admiringly as she watched Vert slip William's dream into the box. Quality-control tags were a way

of checking standards. Once a tagged dream was delivered and in progress, the tag transmitted it back to the screening unit behind the switchboard room. Vert stuck William's order slip onto the top of the box and slid the dream into the warming racks with all the other dreams that were ready for delivery.

"Where are you two off to?" asked Harley as Vert and Midge hurried out of the Dream Kitchens a few minutes later.

Midge turned round. Harley was coming down off the launch pads and walking towards them. Midge started to explain, but then she saw that Snaffle was following Harley. "Us?" said Midge, casually. "Oh, we fancied watching a few dreams. Want to come?"

Snaffle sneered. "Dream watching? What are you, new trainees? I grew out of that in my first week here."

Harley rolled her eyes. "Come on, Snaffle! Anything's better than hanging around with nothing to do. We're waiting for Snaffle's navigation test," she explained to Midge and Vert. "I'm supposed to be going with him. But Team Leader Flint is off on her tea break."

Vert nudged Midge in the ribs and nodded towards the launch pads. The dreamskoot carrying William's dream had just taken off.

"Well," said Midge, watching the dreamskoot pass through the gateway. "We have to go now. Coming?"

"Sure, why not?" said Harley. She walked towards the screening unit with Midge and Vert. "See ya, Snaffle."

"Stupid," muttered Snaffle, watching them go. "So childish." He stood his ground for a few more seconds, then followed Midge, Vert and Harley into the screening unit.

"Split screen?" asked the technician from behind his control desk.

"Yes, please," said Midge. The technician pressed a few buttons and then sat back with his feet up to finish his cup of tea. Midge, Vert, Harley and Snaffle stood in a line in the darkened room, watching a human boy enjoy a flying dream. On one half of the screen, the boy swooped and soared through a bright blue sky. On the other half of the screen, the same boy lay fast asleep in bed.

"Satisfactory," yawned the technician as the flying dream faded from the screen. He pressed another button. Vert nudged Midge. Suddenly they were looking at William Shaw lying in his hospital bed. On the other side of the

screen, the dream had begun. Soft
forgiving music played and gentle
colours swirled comfortingly. Vert
nodded proudly to himself. This was
a good forgiveness dream.

Behind them, the technician began
to snore, lulled to sleep by the music,
but on the screen William frowned. He
shook his head from side to side. The

blips on his heart monitor began to speed up.

"What's happening?" hissed Midge.

Vert bit his lip and looked over his shoulder at the sleeping technician. "The customer is rejecting the dream."

"Why would he do that?" asked Harley.

"He doesn't think he deserves to be forgiven," said Midge, suddenly understanding why William was so upset.

Harley looked puzzled. "But he ordered a forgiveness dream. Didn't he?"

Vert and Midge shared a guilty look. What had they done?

*Blip, blip, blip, blip-blip-blip-BLIP-BLIP-BLIP!* William's heartbeat was racing now.

"This isn't right," said Harley. "I'm going to wake the technician."

"No! Don't do that!" said Midge.

"Why not?" said Snaffle, giving her a suspicious look.

"Because … um…"

*BLIP-BLIP-BLIP-blip-blip, blip, blip, blip. Blip. Blip. Blip.*

Midge heard William's heartbeat slowing back to normal. With a sigh of relief, she looked at the screen. William's eyes were open and he was gazing up at something with a look of great affection.

"…because," continued Midge, "the technician will be mad at you for waking him when there's nothing wrong." She pointed at the screen. "The customer's happy now. See?"

"What's going on?" asked Snaffle. "Something's going on. I can tell."

"Shhh. This is starting to get interesting," said Harley, staring at the screen. "Better than all those swirly, girly colours, anyway."

Vert gave Harley a hurt look. He opened his mouth to defend his dream, but Midge gave him a warning glance. Vert closed his mouth and turned to look at the screen instead. In William's dream, a tall, fair-haired young man in an army uniform had appeared beside the bed. His shirt was open, his sleeves were rolled up and he was laughing down at William.

Midge gasped. "Oh, Vert," she whispered. "You are clever. How did you make him?"

"I didn't make him," hissed Vert, staring at the fair young man. "I just baked a basic forgiveness dream. I don't know where he came from!"

On the screen, William Shaw looked up at the fair-haired young man

 standing by his
bed. "I'm sorry,
James," he said.
"I didn't mean
to leave you
behind. I was just so
frightened. All the sniper fire and the
shells and the dark, dark night…"

William let out a sob and a tear
trickled down his cheek.

"You silly Billy," said James, laughing
down at him. "We all ran! All of us! What
else was there to do? Now, are you ready?"

"What for?" asked William.

"To go," said James, holding out his
hand. "Come on. You'll like it. We're all
there. We've been waiting for such a
long time."

"So have I," sighed William, reaching
out and clasping his friend's hand. "So
have I."

On the hospital side of the screen, a thin old man settled back onto his pillows with a calm smile. On the dream side of the screen, a dark-haired young man climbed from the bed and stood next to James. He was wearing an army uniform. His shirt was open and his sleeves were rolled up. William Shaw grinned and draped an arm over his friend's shoulders. James did the same and, together, they walked out of the dark room and into the light beyond the doors.

*Beeeeeeeeeeeep...*

On the hospital side of the screen, a thin old man lay in his bed, still with a smile of great calm on his face. Beside him, the heart monitor showed a flat line.

"Goodbye, William," whispered Midge.

Beside her, Vert began to mutter in a quavery little voice. "Oh dear. Oh, my.

Oh dear me." This time Midge did not tell him to be quiet.

Harley pulled her mother's kerchief from her neck, clasped it in her fist and held it against her heart. Snaffle stood as straight as he could and gave a smart salute. "Shame," grunted the technician, waking up and looking at the screen. "That William Shaw was a good customer. Still, plenty more where he came from."

"I don't think so," whispered Midge.

# The Cat

**Team Leader Flint** was feeling refreshed and raring to go again after her tea break. She marched along the Dream Centre walkway with a sprightly step, brushing scone crumbs from her front and licking the last of some very tasty clotted cream from her lips.

"Right, Dream Team," she snapped, stepping up onto Snaffle's launch pad.

"Let's get this show on the road. Are you ready for your navigation test, Snaffle?"

"Yes, boss," said Snaffle, standing to attention.

Team Leader Flint gave him a sharp look. He sounded a lot less eager than usual. Was he sickening for something? His ears were decidedly droopy. Harley, Midge and Vert were standing beside Snaffle. Team Leader Flint inspected each of them in turn. Harley had lost her wide smile and Midge and Vert both had red watery eyes.

"All right, trainees," said Team Leader Flint, folding her arms. "What happened while I was on my break?"

"We went to watch a few dreams in the screening unit, boss," began Midge.

"And?"

Midge, Snaffle, Harley and Vert looked at one another.

"Speak up!" snapped Team Leader Flint.

"One of the dreamers – died," said Harley.

"An old male human," added Snaffle.

"We saw it. On the screen," whispered Vert.

"Ah. I see." Team Leader Flint looked at the sad faces of her trainees and decided to try a gentle approach. "Well," she said, awkwardly. "I'm afraid it happens all the time. Can't be helped. And there are more humans being born every second, you know. Still, I can understand how it might upset you..."

Team Leader Flint tailed off. Her trainees were all staring at her as though she had grown an extra nose. What was worse, they were looking even more upset. Hastily, Team Leader Flint abandoned the gentle approach.

"But enough of that!" she snapped briskly. "Snaffle, get your dreamskoot ready for take-off. Harley, you're going with him. Vert, Midge, don't think you can relax just because you have no more flying today. I want your flight reports on my desk within the hour; otherwise I, personally, will tie your ears in knots. Understood?"

"Yes, boss," they chorused, beginning to smile again.

"You think I'm joking?"

"No, boss."

"THEN JUMP TO IT!" bawled Team Leader Flint.

Two minutes later, Snaffle's dreamskoot shot through the gateway and out onto the hilltop above the Earthside town. The dreamskoot slowed to a halt and then began to drift aimlessly above the pile of stones that hid the gateway from human eyes. Snaffle and Harley both sat motionless in the saddle, with identical dazed looks on their faces. They had never experienced such a speedy take-off before. Team Leader Flint had made them do everything in double-quick time and her yells were still ringing in their ears.

Snaffle and Harley raised their helmet visors and took a few calming breaths of night air.

"Where...?" said Harley.

"What…?" said Snaffle.

"Where are we going?" said Harley.

Snaffle shook himself. He had a navigation test to complete. He looked at the delivery details on his tracker screen. "It's a farmhouse."

"Oh, good. A farmhouse doesn't sound too difficult to find," said Harley.

"This one is," said Snaffle, checking his map. "It's a hill farm out in the middle of nowhere. No streetlights. No other buildings. It's the only human place for miles." He looked at the red dot in the far corner of his screen, working out distances in his head. "I'd better get started."

Snaffle took a firm grip on his handlebars and pointed his dreamskoot towards the dark hills on the western horizon. Harley watched the moonlit fields skim past below them.

"This is peaceful," she said. "It's good to get away from old Flint Face for a while. She was starting to give me a headache."

"You shouldn't talk about our Team Leader like that," sniffed Snaffle.

"Why?" drawled Harley. "Are you planning to tell tales on me too?"

"I was not telling tales on Vert! I was making my report."

"You were trying to knock Vert out of first place," said Harley. "Didn't work though, did it? Fifty points, Snaffle. You gave Vert fifty extra points!"

Snaffle scowled.

"I wish you wouldn't keep trying to sabotage the rest of us," sighed Harley. "It's not right."

"There's nothing wrong with a bit of competition!" said Snaffle.

"It's not right," insisted Harley. "We're a

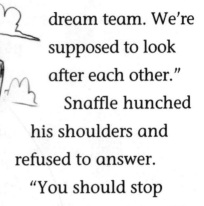

dream team. We're supposed to look after each other."

Snaffle hunched his shoulders and refused to answer.

"You should stop trying so hard," said Harley softly.

"What are you talking about?" sneered Snaffle.

"You should stop trying to be like your brother. You're not Grabble. You're Snaffle! If your mum and dad can't like you for who you are, then they're not worth bothering about."

"And what would you know about parents?" hissed Snaffle.

Harley gasped and fell silent. Snaffle felt bad. He wanted to say sorry, but his pride would not let him. Instead, he whistled a tune to show that he did not care.

The farmhouse was hidden in a high
valley that was little more than a crease
in the skin of the land. By the time
Snaffle found it, his teeth were chattering
so much he could not whistle any more.
Up in the high hills the wind was
freezing. Frost glittered on the humped
backs of dry-stone walls. Hillside streams
rattled over the rocks with a sharp, cold
sound like ice cubes in a glass.

Snaffle was also feeling the chill from

Harley. She had sat behind him, silent and icy, all through the long climb up into the hills. Even the customized saddle-warmer on Snaffle's dreamskoot had failed to thaw her out. As they hovered above the glittering slates of the farmhouse roof, Snaffle opened his mouth to say sorry. But again his pride would not let him. He kept his silence and brought up a three-dimensional plan of the farmhouse on his tracker screen.

"The customer is in a first-floor bedroom at the back of the house, in case you're interested," he said casually.

No reply.

Snaffle began to feel annoyed. Who did Harley think she was, freezing him out like this over one little comment? He wrenched the handlebars of his dreamskoot towards the back of the house. The little machine skimmed down the slope of the roof, out over the guttering and into the farmyard. Snaffle hovered while he surveyed the back of the house. His customer's bedroom window was the middle one of three. It was an old, wooden sash window. The bottom half was propped open with a brick.

Snaffle smiled. How convenient. He headed for the open window but stopped before he reached it. He had suddenly remembered the little safety rhyme all Dream Fetchers were taught.

*Makes you shiver? Don't deliver.*

Something about the open window was making Snaffle shiver. Why would a window be propped open with a brick on a night as cold as this? Snaffle double-checked his delivery details. The dream had been ordered by a thirteen-year-old human called Ben. Snaffle nodded wisely. He had read all about teenage boys. They had sweaty armpits and smelly feet. They liked to grow mould in mugs. They kept old slices of pizza under their beds and never put their underpants in the wash. No wonder this human boy had the window wedged open. His bedroom must smell really bad.

Snaffle eased into the room. The curtains were not closed, and moonlight shone in through the window. Ben was snoring under a pile of clothes, chocolate wrappers and magazines. Snaffle looked around, ticking items off as he spotted them. "Dirty underpants? Check. Mouldy mugs? Check. Old pizza? Extremely." Snaffle relaxed. As far as he was concerned, the open window was explained. He turned to pull the dream box from its holder. A silent Harley was already holding it out to him. Snaffle took it from her without a word, zoomed in on the bed and made the drop.

*Phut!* The dream landed on Ben's shoulder and sank into him. Snaffle turned away from the bed just as the real reason for the open window poked its head out from the bottom of Ben's duvet...

A cat. A big, muscled tomcat. A hunter.

The cat yawned as it emerged from its favourite sleeping place, showing all its sharp white fangs. Snaffle and Harley were heading for the window. They did not see the cat, but the cat saw them. Instantly it was wide awake. In one smooth motion, the cat went into a crouch and sprang at the little dreamskoot. Snaffle and Harley were completely unaware of the clawed menace flying towards them. They ducked under the

window-frame and
floated off over the
farmyard a microsecond
before the cat landed on
the windowsill behind
them. A paw armed
with claws as

sharp as
scalpels tried to
hook them back, but
the dreamskoot was just out of
reach. The cat gave a silent snarl and
dug its claws into the wooden window
frame instead. Its prey had escaped.

Snaffle and Harley had no idea how
lucky they had just been. Snaffle began to
make a leisurely turn above the farmyard
so that he could hop over the roof of the
house and head off down the valley.

*Whoohoo-hoo, whoohoo-hoo.*

The noise made Snaffle's hair stand up in frightened spikes under his helmet. Somewhere above him, an owl was hunting. Snaffle had been carried off by an owl during his first solo flight. Now all the terror came flooding back. Snaffle panicked. He put his dreamskoot into a dive so steep that even Harley was frightened.

All Snaffle could think about was getting away from the owl. As his dreamskoot plunged towards the farmyard, he was looking up at the sky.

"Pull up, Snaffle!" cried Harley, thumping him on the back. "Pull up!"

Snaffle tore his gaze away from the sky and looked down. The ridged concrete of the farmyard was rushing towards him. He yanked on his handlebars. The dreamskoot shuddered and slowed but its nose was not coming up. Snaffle tilted the dreamskoot, trying to catch some wind resistance. The wings began to vibrate so much that they made an eerie wailing sound. Slowly, slowly, his dreamskoot pulled out of the dive and levelled out centimetres above the concrete.

Snaffle came to a halt and hovered just above the ground while he checked out the sky. Behind him, the cat slid from the windowsill like a length of black silk and landed lightly on the little porch roof above the back door of the farmhouse.

"Snaffle," hissed Harley. "We're too low."

"I'm not going any higher," said Snaffle, looking for a dark, winged shape against the stars. "There's an owl. Didn't you hear?"

The cat flowed from the porch roof onto the water barrel and then down to the ground.

"Even if there was an owl, it's probably in the next valley by now," said Harley. "We're in more danger down here than in the sky. This is a farmyard, Snaffle. All sorts of things could be stalking us." Harley checked the shadows to her left. "A fox, for instance." She scanned the big barn on her right. "Or a weasel. A rat," she continued, turning to look over her shoulder. "Or a – CAT!" screamed Harley, her voice full of terror. "CAT!"

Snaffle reacted swiftly. He opened the throttle and shot forward just as the stalking cat pounced. He looked over his shoulder and saw a nightmare of teeth and claws flying towards him. With a gasp he pushed his dreamskoot to the limit and pointed it skyward.

*Slam!*

The cat had stretched out a paw in mid-leap and batted them out of the air. Dreamskoot and cat fell to the concrete together. The cat hissed as its prey skittered away across the farmyard like a skimmed pebble. Snaffle and Harley hung on and hoped the dreamskoot would stay upright. Miraculously, it did. They came to a stop in front of the barn.

"In there!" cried Harley, pointing to a gap at the bottom of one of the doors. The cat was nearly upon them as Snaffle shot through the gap and into the dark barn. He flicked on his headlight and turned the dreamskoot in a full circle, looking for a hiding place. Two horses snorted in their stalls as the headlight beam passed over them. A tractor and a quad bike sat in the middle of the barn. A hen coop stood against the far wall.

A hiss made Snaffle turn to face the doors again. The cat was squeezing itself through the gap. It turned its huge, scarred head towards them and snarled. Its eyes were silver discs in the headlight beam. Its black fur glinted like oil.

"It's a monster," whimpered Snaffle. He was frozen with fear.

"Move!" yelled Harley.

Snaffle moved. He headed for the hen coop. The cat lashed out and clipped the back of the dreamskoot as it zipped past. Snaffle was nearly flung from the saddle. Grimly, he clung onto the handlebars

and steered his dreamskoot
into the safety of the hen coop.

*Squawk! Bwuark! Flap-a-flap-a-flap!*
*Squawk! Bwuark!*

Snaffle flew into an explosion of
feathers. Panicked hens flapped and
scrambled all around the dreamskoot.
Hastily, Snaffle folded away the delicate
silver wings.

*Poing! Skrittle! Skrattle! Poing!*

Some hens aimed panicked pecks at
his helmet, and others scraped it with
their scaly feet as they scrambled away.

A few shot out of the hen house, only to shoot back in again when they saw the cat outside. Snaffle backed the dreamskoot into a corner and then cowered in the mess of straw and bird droppings on the floor.

Finally the hens began to settle down again. They all squashed into the other end of the hen house, clucking disapprovingly. Their beady eyes glittered in the headlight beam as they jerked their heads this way and that.

"What is it with me and birds?" said Snaffle with a shaky laugh.

No answer.

Snaffle sighed. Harley really was taking her sulk too far. "It pongs a bit in here, doesn't it?"

No answer.

"So. What do we do, Harley? Sit it out until the cat leaves?"

Still no answer. Snaffle checked his dreamcom. It was definitely working. He lost his patience. "What are you playing at?" he demanded, twisting round to glare at Harley. The saddle behind him was empty. Snaffle felt his heart plunge into his boots. His eyes widened with horror.

"Harley?" He checked the straw all around him. Harley was not there. Snaffle remembered the cat clipping the back of his dreamskoot just before he reached the safety of the hen house. He had only managed to stay in the saddle by hanging onto the handlebars. Harley must have been thrown off. He had left her out in the barn. With the cat.

"Harley?" he said into his dreamcom. "Can you hear me? Where are you?"

Silence.

"Come in, Harley. Please…"

There was no reply. Snaffle eased his dreamskoot up to the doorway of the hen house. He peered outside. The cat was lying on the barn floor beside the horse stalls. It was holding something between its front paws. As Snaffle watched, the cat dipped its head. Snaffle heard the crunch of bones. Suddenly, he could not watch any more. He backed away from the door, wrapped his arms around himself and rocked back and forth. "I'm sorry, Harley," he whispered, too late. "I'm sorry."

Alone in the smelly darkness, Snaffle cried.

The horse pushed its whiskery muzzle into the feeding trough and took a mouthful of hay. Its big square teeth chomped together centimetres from Harley's head. She gave a muffled squeak and burrowed down further into the trough. At first, Harley had thought she had been lucky to make such a soft landing after being thrown from the dreamskoot. Now she was not so sure.

Harley peered out between the planks of the feeding trough. The cat was right above her, prowling along the top of the stall wall. It knew she was in here somewhere. Harley would have to stay absolutely still and silent until the cat gave up. She reached up to her helmet and turned off her dreamcom. At least Snaffle had made it to safety. Harley could see the faint glow of his dreamskoot headlight inside the hen coop.

*Harrummphhh!*

The horse's muzzle appeared again, blasting Harley with warm, hay-smelling air. The lips pulled back. The big square teeth came towards her. Harley ducked. *Chomp!* Another mouthful of hay disappeared.

Harley scrambled back to the gap between the planks and looked out. The cat was staring at something on the floor of the stall. Harley looked too. The straw was moving slightly. As she watched, a mouse popped its head out of the straw and looked around with its whiskers twitching. It spotted the cat and shot away under the door of the stall. The cat jumped after the mouse and disappeared from sight. A second later, Harley heard a high squeak. Now was her chance to escape, but she would have to move fast. A mouse snack would not keep the cat busy for long.

Harley scrambled out of the feeding trough and began to climb the wooden wall of the stall. As she pulled herself from nail to knothole, she kept looking over her shoulder. If the cat appeared now, she would be finished. Harley reached the top of the stall wall and hauled herself onto the narrow ledge. The cat was on the barn floor directly below her. It had something between its paws. Harley swallowed and looked away. She switched her dreamcom back on.

"Snaffle," she whispered.

"Harley! You're alive!"

"Shhhh. The cat is right below me, eating a poor mouse."

"I thought it was eating you!" wailed Snaffle.

"No. I'm up on the wall of the horse's stall. Can you see me?"

The glow of light from the dreamskoot headlight brightened as Snaffle moved into the doorway of the hen coop. "Yes. I can see you."

"OK. Here's what we do..."

A few seconds later, Snaffle eased his dreamskoot out of the hen coop and worked his way around the edge of the barn. The urge to go faster was very strong, but Snaffle kept to a crawl. As long as he let the dreamskoot idle along, the engine would stay as quiet as a whisper.

He reached the tractor without being seen and peeked out from behind the huge black tyre. The cat was still busy with the mouse. Snaffle looked up at the stall. Harley was crouched on the top of the wall, waiting for him.

Snaffle swallowed hard and forced himself to leave the shelter of the tractor. This was the most dangerous part. He was flying out in the open, right in front of the cat. He had nearly reached the stall when a stray moonbeam lit up the silvery wings of his dreamskoot. The cat raised its head and looked right at him.

Snaffle opened the throttle. His dreamskoot surged forward. Below him the cat left the remains of the mouse and jumped up onto the top of the stall. The cat saw Harley and began to stalk towards her. Harley backed away from it. Snaffle heard her terrified whimper in the earpiece of his dreamcom.

"Hold on, Harley!" he yelled, driving his dreamskoot between Harley and the cat. The cat and Harley both sprang towards him. The dreamskoot rocked as Harley landed on her front across the saddle and then Snaffle shot away again a split second before the cat slammed down on top of them. Harley scrambled into a sitting position behind Snaffle as he sped across the barn. The cat yowled as it raced after them. Snaffle shuddered at the sound. He coaxed more speed out of his dreamskoot. He had to reach the gap in the barn door ahead of the cat!

The cat yowled again, much closer now. Snaffle aimed his dreamskoot at the gap and shot through just as the cat thudded into the door behind them.

Snaffle and Harley lifted their helmet visors and took deep gulps of the cold night air as the dreamskoot soared up into the sky. They could not quite believe they had survived. Neither of them said a word as Snaffle flew over the farmhouse roof and headed off down the valley.

"I don't like cats," said Harley, after a while.

Snaffle gave a shout of laughter that turned into a sob. "I thought

you were dead!" he cried.

"I'm sorry, Snaffle," said Harley. "I had to turn off my dreamcom in case the cat heard something. Thanks for rescuing me. You were very brave, flying right in front of it like that."

"The whole thing was my fault, though," admitted Snaffle. "If I hadn't flown so low across the farmyard to start with—"

"Doesn't matter," said Harley. "We made it. And, hey! You passed your navigation test!"

"You mean—" Snaffle hesitated. "You mean you're not going to report me to

Team Leader Flint for flying too low?"

"How many times?" sighed Harley. "We're a dream team, Snaffle. In my book, that means we're a family. I'm not going to tell on you."

"Oh." Snaffle flew on in silence for a while. "Harley?"

"Yes?"

"I won't do it any more."

"What?"

"I won't try to sabotage you or Midge or Vert any more. I'm still going to aim for the highest score in the team. But no sabotage. I promise."

Harley was silent for a long time. Snaffle scowled. Why didn't she say something? Did she realize how much it had cost him to make that promise?

"Have you switched off your dreamcom again?" he demanded.

Harley still said nothing, but she slid

her arms around Snaffle's waist and gave him a fierce hug. Snaffle felt his heart fill up with startled happiness.

"Girls," he sneered. "Talk about soft."

But when Harley kept her arms around his waist all the way back to Dreamside, Snaffle did not protest once.

"Relax, kiddo," drawled Harley. "Flying solo is no big deal."

But for tiny Dream Fetchers, going solo is not the only worry on a first Earthside mission. Whatever happens, they mustn't break the Three Abiding Rules:

1: Always deliver what the customer orders
2: Don't look inside the box
3: Never be seen

Could Midge's first dream delivery also be her last?

# DreamTeam

"your dreams delivered"

Look out for the
Dream Team as
they return in …

## Mission 3:
## Speed Challenge

## Mission 4:
## Daydream Shift